Worcestershire Young Writer Competition Anthology

Edited by Black Pear Press

With contributions by the entrants in the 2016
Worcestershire Literary Festival and Titania,
supported by Rotary, Young Writer Competition

Thanks and acknowledgements to Judges:
Prof. Rod Griffiths
Dr. Tony Judge
Rtn. Mary Nettle
and to the moderator:
Rtn. Polly Stretton

This anthology is brought to you by
The Worcestershire LitFest & Fringe
Young Writer Team www.worcslitfest.co.uk

Black Pear Press

Lucid
Worcestershire Young Writer Competition Anthology 2016

First published in October 2016 by Black Pear Press
www.blackpear.net

Compiled & edited by:
Black Pear Press

ISBN 978-1-910322-37-6
Cover Design by Black Pear Press

Introduction

This anthology is created from the entries for The Worcestershire Literary Festival (LitFest) and Titania, Rotary in Great Britain & Ireland, Young Writer Competition 2016. Competition entrants submitted stories of up to 300 words based on their choice from two themes *Apocalypse* or *Utopia*, which could be written about separately or together, selected by our sponsor, Titania.

Rotary In Great Britain & Ireland (RGBI) run a Young Writer Competition in the final quarter of each year. Rotarians have assisted LitFest and Titania with this summer competition for the past three years. We, at Black Pear Press, were delighted to be asked to support the organisations in this endeavour.

The judges said that they were most impressed by the quality of the entries and said there were clever entries dealing with the destructive side of human nature with eloquent and convincing dialogue, entertaining yet mature in approach. Also, those young writers who attempted to write about both topics were successful in moving from one to the other. There were a few grammatical lapses and some overuse of adjectives, but overall lots of imaginative and readable work.

Editing is something that most writers are apprehensive about, and when it comes to editing young writers' work it has to be done with particular care and consideration. We trust that the edits in this anthology will be seen as improvements and to have been done with empathy and sensitivity. For the most part the edits were limited to spelling and punctuation.

Black Pear Press Limited

Competition Winners

The Worcestershire Literary Festival Young Writer Team and Titania announced the winning entries at the launch of the Worcestershire Literary Festival 2016 with representatives from Rotary taking part.

The shortlisted entries in the competition were (alphabetical order):

Sarah Adegbite *the boy whose jeans were made of oceans*
Lizzie Austen *Lucid*
Vilmos Borodi *Apocalypse*
Edie Callanan *The Seasons Have Won*
Martha Davey *Apocalypse*
Charlie Johns *Utopia*
Erkia Jones *Apocalypse*
Abby Trow *Utopia*
Olivia Sproule *From Utopia To Apocalypse*

These stories are the first nine in this anthology followed by entries selected by the editors.

The winners in each category were:
Senior 14-17
Lizzie Austen—John Masefield High School

Intermediate 11-13
Abby Trow—King's Hawford School

Junior 7-10
Martha Davey—King's Hawford School

Contents

Short Listed Entries

Lucid – Lizzie Austen

Behind her back, Rowan constructed her city. For weeks on end she had worked on it; she had perfected every single detail.

She turned and faced her Utopia.

Well, almost.

Here, there was no graffiti. The streets were clean, and there was no crime. It was, quite literally, a dream world.

However, Rowan was frustrated with her work. It wasn't right. She always needed to tweak it.

But today, something was amiss.

She didn't recognise this one.

He sat atop the wall to her left, his heel thumping an irregular rhythm on the red bricks. As he turned to face her, his eyes sparkled in the sunlight.

'Hello.'

Rowan was momentarily dumbstruck. They weren't supposed to speak.

The stranger ceased the tapping.

'Are you ready?' He asked.

'What?' She blanched. 'Ready for what? What do you mean?'

He released a long, heavy sigh.

'Ah, so blind that you can't see what it is you truly want. It gets very tiresome, Rowan.'

She chose to ignore the fact that he knew her name.

'What are you doing in my dream?' She spoke with as much force as she could muster.

'*Your* dream, is it? Just because you realised where you are doesn't suddenly make it *your* dream. Without me, you wouldn't be here.'

Rowan's brow furrowed. 'So, you're my... subconscious?'

'Bravo,' he said, clapping slowly. 'I'm here to fix your city.'

Her eyes widened. 'You can?'

'Certainly,' he smirked. 'Just look.'

Without warning, the paving slabs below began to split. The skyscrapers roared, metal twisting, glass shattering into shards.

'No!' She shrieked.

The grin widened. 'We all have flaws. It's human nature. And designing this without all those mistakes? It doesn't sit well. So, we bring the other thing that humans excel at.' He glanced at her tear-stained face.

'Apocalypse.'

Utopia – Abby Trow

The doctor's words echoed through Debbie's head.

'I'm so sorry, survival rates are low. Just five per cent last over a year.'

'Me, a terminal illness; this just can't be happenin',' she thought.

Deborah Manson was at the top of her modelling career, living the lifestyle others could only dream about. Beautiful clothes, exotic destinations, expensive jewellery, rich and famous friends…she had it all.

Debbie had two loving parents, and her upbringing had been good. She was blessed with beauty and elegance, coming from her mother's side. With such good parents and genes, stardom beckoned her.

However, her career turned her into a rather spoilt, attention-seeking diva. The more the success, the more disgraceful the behaviour. She soon became known for her tantrums as much as her looks. Life to her was simply about image; how she looked, what she was wearing and who she was with.

All was to change in April 2010. For this was when she was diagnosed with a terminal illness. There was little hope of surviving beyond twelve months.

It is at moments like these that people can change. For Debbie this is exactly what happened. The little girl, from that loving family, came back to life; and so did her fighting spirit.

'I'll be one of the five per cent that survive,' she thought.

Six years on and Debbie sits in her overgrown garden, wearing scruffy jeans, an old jumper, and a pair of well-used flip-flops. With her eyes shut and

5

head resting back, the sun glows gently on her face. A warm breeze carries a waft of roses. Only the gentle hum of bees can be heard.

Debbie gently squeezes her mother's hand as she thinks:

'I'm alive. This is what life is really about. This is my Utopia.'

Apocalypse – Martha Davey

A mist hung low over the deserted space, smothering the world like a thick, woollen blanket. Sky the colour of a raging sea, bellowed and roared above; a distant jay gave one last 'caw' and flapped slowly off. The smell of noxious chemicals curled into his nostrils. He shivered as a river of cold sweat slithered down his pale cheek. It was a cataclysmic scene—why had this fatal thing been bestowed on him, why?

Distraught, he trudged into the nearest dilapidated ruin of a building and slumped down in the far corner. 'What will happen to me?' moaned the boy. His chin dropped even lower and he found himself staring at his hands, hoping that the answer might be there. He felt as if there was nothing to do and nothing to be said in this calamitous world. 'How can I get out of this?' he pondered in desperation. 'If only I had concentrated, this would never have happened,' he murmured to himself. 'How will I survive?' he yelled, a demon suddenly released inside him. 'Why didn't I use my common sense, now look what I've got myself into!'

He started to ferociously yank his coal-black hair, ripping out numerous strands. His eyes glowed with rage. His knuckles whitened, clamped into a fist, and he was seized by a sudden urge to take his anger out on something; he began thumping the wall so hard that a thin crack sped vertically to the ceiling. It was like watching a child being punished with a vicious cane—Tyson Fury would have been impressed.

'Stop hitting the wall, boy!' came a voice from the gloom. 'You've just forgotten your swimming kit, it's really not the end of the world.'

Cogitations – Charlie Johns

Plato placed his thumb and forefinger upon his glabella and closed his eyes in rumination.

Hunching forward slightly, he brought his forehead down upon his knee and furrowed his brow.

'Utopia…Utopia…' he murmured.

Alone in his sanctum, Plato's eyes screwed shut with the mental strain of contemplating the existence of a perfect society. He'd answered many great questions in his lifetime: the meaning of life, mankind's place in the cosmos; but he couldn't lug his enormous brain around the issue of a utopian paradise.

His vocal chords, responsible for some of the most profound words ever uttered, were reduced to grunts of intellectual frustration. Perhaps there was no solution to this theoretical pandemonium.

A marble bust of Socrates looked down on him with a mocking expression. For a moment Plato marvelled at the thickness of his beard and then chastised his inner metrosexual.

Young Aristotle entered the room with a plate of lemon drizzle for his master, and, seeing him doubled over on the floor gazing into Socrates' face, was disquieted.

'Is this a good time?' inquired Aristotle.

'Boy,' Plato drawled, turning to face the student with bloodshot eyes, stray locks of hair plastered to his drenched face. 'What is the perfect society?'

'Isn't it for everyone to be happy?' Aristotle chirped. 'Do you want this cake?'

'Idiot child! Leave now,' slurred Plato, theatrically knocking the sponge to the floor with a sweep of the hand. As Aristotle departed, Plato knelt on the floor, contemplating the boy's words as the neurones in his brain unravelled a knot of the esoteric conundrum.

'Hmm...' he murmured as he scribbled down Aristotle's thesis for further contemplation. He turned to face snide Socrates. 'Go away, old man. You're dead now.'

Or was he?

Plato hunched over. 'Hmm...the continued existence of the soul...'

Apocalypse – Erika Jones

It is now five minutes since my whole life changed before my eyes.

The day was going so well, or as well as it could when there is a war going on around you. At least then I had some of my family, now I have no one, no one at all. There are not many survivors. I've only seen one other like me all alone with no one to talk to. It is like a ghost town here, no colour, no laughter, no happiness, no nothing. The only thing that is left is rubble. The bomb just had to hit our town. If it weren't for that, I would still have my mum and my dad and everyone else I cared for and loved. I remember all of the really fun things I used to do with my family, all the trips we use to go on. Now I guess none of that is ever going to happen again.

I remember the stories my father used to tell me, now I have none of that. I can't even picture it; all I can see in my mind is darkness no happiness; it's black and grey and miserable. When I used to be miserable or sad my little sister used to cheer me up, but I guess she is gone now so there is no use thinking of her doing that for me anymore. My father always used to tell me to stay positive even when it gets tough. I never really understood what he meant, but now I think I know what he was trying to say. He was talking about times like now when I am alone and my whole life has just been destroyed. I guess now I am alone I will have to take into account what my father said and stay strong.

From Utopia To Apocalypse – Olivia Sproule

Dear Diary,

Another perfect day, the burning sun has risen and set. I am sitting on a cosy carpet of leaves inside my family's hut, full of anticipation, as tomorrow is my tenth birthday. Finally, I shall be allowed to take on senior responsibilities for my tribe. Daily from dawn, I will walk to our mellifluous stream and collect water to drink; this duty will be a tremendous honour for me. My birthday.

Today I became ten! I awoke excitedly and raced outside. Grabbing the empty ancient pot from beside the fire, I carefully balanced it on top of my head and skipped blissfully to the stream. I smiled as our source of life twisted, turned, bubbled and gurgled on its journey through our village, before plunging my vessel into its depths and filling it to the brim with clear, fresh water. Ambling back home I was in heaven allowing the earth's cool mud to squelch between the toes of my bare feet.

Suddenly my joyfulness changed to trepidation as a mass of yellow mountainous mechanical monsters swarmed towards our village like a pack of oversized angry bees, their buzz magnified. Running for our lives, my tribe and I sprinted into the jungle in fear. We watched, helpless, as these humongous creatures trampled over our Utopia, instantly destroying everything in their path. We crouched in terror as the beasts breathed fire over our huts, filled our beloved stream with dust, flattened our beautiful flora and knocked down age-old trees like a pack of playing cards.

I felt dizzy. I did not understand. My head hurt. The container of water had remained intact in its new home on top of my head. As I closed my eyes its contents dripped down my face, joining my tears, in unison, mourning this Apocalypse.

the boy whose jeans were made of oceans
– Sarah Adegbite

12.04.3002

it was at this wretched moment in time that i realised the depth of trouble we had swum into: my brother was about to do the most idiotic thing in the history of idiocy, and i had to be the one to stop him. the streets are paved with blood, and only heroes run onto it barefoot.

'no! jed---come back!' the words had barely escaped before he started off; faded jeans swished like ocean ripples as he shot into the chaos. a child's scream summoned my brother's lionheart help, and streaked skies stared down at me. tears slithered through the grime on my face.

'get back here! get back here or…or...' he may have been an idiot, but he was fearless. stumbling after him, balls of terror were lodged in my throat, breathing felt like swallowing sulphuric clouds. jedidiah had headed for the twelve-storey across the street. it was a palm tree, swaying in apocalyptic winds, *the breath of irrevocable destruction.*

'jed! where are you?'

a faint cry from the roof managed to swirl its way down. i could see a blurred outline, a hand in the air, a movement. *thank God, he was safe.* a shaved cat lay writhing on the floor, eyes bulging, and i vomited my pain next to it, storming up the stairs. up, up, stair upon stair, bursting out onto the roof. *hot air bellowed at me, and i shouted back:*

'jed! jed!' he wasn't here. i sprinted lead legs to the roof's edge, and time slowed. down. he lay, sprawled amongst apocalypse, concrete cracks, the sharp, slate bricks of homes, and blood. *blood?* his jeans were scarred, stained, brown more than blue. they looked like oceans that had ceased to ripple; drained of all water, *all life.*

Apocalypse – Vilmos Borodi

Glass shattered everywhere, an ear-piercing noise. I manage to stand up. I didn't hear any crying or screaming. I looked out one more time. Then the plane exploded…

I crash-landed in a ghostly abandoned city. I'm the only survivor.

I have to repeat this in my mind to make sure I wasn't badly hurt. Everything seems cold and quiet and I know straight away that I have to make it through this city or I will have no chance of surviving. As I walk along the wet gravel I scarcely make out a figure walking towards me. My trembling feet make their way towards it and I know at once it must be hostile. I quickly grab a sharp stick from the wet pavement and start charging towards it. We touch at the same time. Slowly all dies down and I know it's safe to get up.

The weather is grey—black clouds looming over the eerie place and me. The silence is haunting. No one moves except me, like this city was never known. The pungent smell of the smoke from a building makes me hold my breath, tingling my nostrils

I hope nobody is watching, spying on me. Who made the plane crash? Anger fills me. On the horizon, another figure runs towards me. When it approaches closer, I can make out it is a human. His face is streaked with blood mixed with mud. I get ready. But he doesn't attack. All he says is 'You ain't getting out of this place! Nobody can!.' And then he drops down on the floor—dead. I gulp. I'm already starting to realise, this jungle of a city is endless.

This is the end.

The Seasons Have Won – Edie Callanan

The seasons were happy. They had conspired to destroy the world and kill humankind and knew that if they used their powers in unity they would be unstoppable!

Summer's great power came from her ability to control the sun. She began her assault on Earth by directing the sun onto Antarctica, causing the ice to melt. Water levels rose, meaning coastal areas worldwide flooded.

Autumn's lungs were enormous and she used her breath like the wind to create tsunamis, causing destruction and distress in her wake.

Weather reporters across the world were confused and even the science community were baffled by the strange happenings. People were terrified, fearing for their lives and fleeing their homes.

The seasons relished seeing the broken families and the damage they had done. Summer was feeling especially proud of herself and continued to spit fireballs at famous landmarks. She considered these her little present to Earth.

Spring was supposed to symbolise new life, but she was doing the exact opposite. Using her signature poisonous flower, that was deadly enough to kill with one sniff, she wiped out a whole city. She also sent mutant vines, winding them around people and cars, crushing and strangling them.

The final group of survivors were wiped out, except for a teenage girl. Tears pricked her eyes and she willed herself to be strong until the very end. She watched without fear as Winter cut a shard of ice and sent it flying, cutting through the air as it soared before penetrating her heart. The last thing she saw was blood as she took her final breath. She fell to the floor with a soft thud.

It Rained That Day – Flora Barber

It rained that day. I guess I shouldn't have been surprised given the news, but I never thought the sky would actually commit an act of pathetic fallacy. Those things only happen in films and fairy tales, I told myself, not in real life. Yet no matter how much I wished it was just a bad dream, I knew deep inside that this sick bitter taste drying and infecting my mouth was real. The rain had scratched at my face, but even that pain had not surpassed or blinded me against this numbness clawing its burning melancholy inside of me. I cried and screamed and ranted my rage, but this internal war was silent, undetectable to the world outside. Perhaps, if you'd looked close enough, you would have caught a glimpse of it breaching into the shape of a furrowed brow on my forehead. Or maybe you'd encounter the blood seeping through the battlefield in my eyes and find the shadows marking the hours I lay awake for fear of those fitful dreams where you were still beside me, holding my hand, kissing my cheek; but those memories are gone, and so are you. The Apocalypse is not some Hollywood set rigged up in a computer, but the personal battle you fight trying to survive when you've lost the people you love. It's the hours and days, the months and years you have to live without them. Time heals wounds, not people. When all of your friends are dead, your family buried, and there's nobody left, what are you but a piece of rock carved into with words that mean nothing anymore. You are just a story lost to the breeze, like ashes in the mist, and you are gone. You are gone and I am alone once more.

The Dark Side Of Heaven – Louis Hira

I kick myself every day. Thousands were killed, two were to blame. Isn't it obvious that those two master criminals would be somewhere along the snaking line of heaven hopefuls?

The guard got bored observing 'innocent' after 'innocent' on his screen, everyone seemed worthy of heaven. Little did he know that his one push of a button would turn a peaceful paradise into utter madness.

The two slimy individuals that slipped beneath the radar were brothers, Leroy and Raj Pickering. They had suicidally bombed the 2024 football world cup final. It was a diabolical plan: first football, then heaven.

Once in, the twisted pair used heaven's marvellous duplicating machinery to make catastrophic clones of themselves. Each one shared the same muscular body and destructive thoughts. An army of despicable, frightening human beings were slowly tearing the Utopia apart. People tried to stop them, but what could they do? If they used violence in heaven they risked being banished forever. All they could do was watch as their beloved homes, favourite places, and beautiful gardens were demolished.

Within minutes, heaven had turned into hell: the fiery, endless abyss of darkness, all because of one careless guard. A place, once so full of life and happiness, had become a blazing inferno full of misery and shattered dreams.

Twelve years have passed and nothing has changed, apart from one thing: there is no more heaven. Just a massive pile of burning rubble, thousands of terrified . humans, and millions of destructive brutes.

Now do you see my point? Why I'm eternally in despair? I have nothing to live for, nothing to hope for. My pitiful existence may as well be stricken from the record books because I am a failure. Oh, and in case you haven't realised, I was the guard.

Young Writers aged 7-10

Apocalypse – Ben Hone

How does a nuclear power station work? It is a lot easier to understand if you call the neutron A and the uranium nucleus B. A hits B. B splits, releasing more A. Repeat. All the time this produces energy. Scientists have been trying to achieve a more efficient way of making energy for years. And finally they have found one. Nuclear fusion: the act of joining smaller nuclei to effectively make a bigger one. Since the sea provides the hydrogen isotopes needed, the length of this process is almost limitless. But there's a catch. You need a lot of heat. By the year 2040, we were still trying. By the year 2041, we'd done it. Anything can be done with a deep pocket and dreams I suppose.

Can't it?

In acceptance of the cliché, it was a normal summer's day. The sun had reduced everything to a dehydrated mess; water bottles were empty and you could only lap the stuff, which may as well have been poisonous for all you care, out of the tap.

This was exactly how Mark Banks felt, except there was no tap in sight. He was trundling along in his '85 Alfa Romeo GTV6 in the middle of nowhere. His heart plummeted as he saw something quite simply disgusting there—and he vowed never to drive down that road again. Six great cooling towers formed a circle around a huge reactor, a jumble of pipes and turbines. When a whir started to emit from the machine, he frowned. Which was rare for such an optimist. Then something terrible happened. A huge sphere of light expanded from the centre of the nuclear power station, and Mark barely had time to pinch himself to see if he was dreaming before death had enveloped him.

Utopia – Amelia Lees

Is this a dream? Am I awake? Where am I? I'm confused. Suddenly, I see something and I can't quite work out what it is. I rub my eyes in disbelief, as this is definitely not my bedroom.

I find myself in an unbelievably comfortable bed that is big and luxurious—just like floating on a big fluffy cloud on a clear sunny day. There are maids carrying trays brimming with delicious food filling the air with sweet lovely smells. Also surrounding me are beautiful pink flamingos dancing beside magnificent ballerinas leaping through the air. I turn my head, struggling to take everything in and see the biggest chocolate fountain complete with oodles of toppings and heaps of fruit, delicious!

All of a sudden I heard a loud knock at the door. Everything stopped and there was horrible silence. Who could it be? What is about to happen in this world of happiness and paradise? A tiny fairy came rushing through the gap in the door and flew straight at me. She was very excited and asked me to dance.

She took my hand and as I climbed out of the bed, the flamingos started to bow their heads and the ballerinas curtsied. The music started to play and everyone got into position. I began to smile as we all began to dance, with beautiful, flowing moves and spins. We created rainbows as we leapt across the stage. After hours of dancing I felt so exhausted and fell backwards onto the soft bed. I struggled to keep my eyes open and drifted off straight to sleep.

I heard the rain hitting the windows; I opened my eyes and I was back in my bedroom. I looked out of the window and wished to be back in that bright, wonderful world soon.

Apocalypse to Utopia – Amy Hall

Dear Diary
19th June 2050
It's been five months to the day now since they came.
Every day more and more people die. I don't get it.
Why are they killing people for fun? We never did
anything to them. Whenever I look out of my one-
windowed safe house at the scenes, I don't believe that
I'm still in Liverpool. I know that the fight is
happening everywhere but we surely are having the
worst of it.

The once mighty Anfield is lying in ruins, no more
churches, there's no communication anymore, they
snapped all the wires. When they aren't attacking
people wonder the streets with forlorn expressions not
talking. There are no men left in the city that can fight.
We've done our part in this defence for our country.
Even I kicked one in the head! It's the rest of the
world not doing their job and we can't hold out much
longer.

Lucy Mallark

Dear Diary
19th September 2052

It's been two years since they left. Things are back to
normal. The flowers and bushes are in full bloom and
there are more men on the streets. The first day when
the sun came up was the best day of my life. Flowers
sprang out of the earth and the birds sang again. By
popular demand a shop called THEMKILLER is still

around, they literally simulate if you have managed to defeat one of them. Guess what, I succeeded!

Tomorrow is the first day back at school and I can't wait to see Flo, Alicia, Michaela and Amy, I can't wait to see all of them.

But we have just heard that my daddy is lost and may never turn back up...but you never know...

Lucy Mallark

Utopia – Bea Morgan

Jonny hated mistakes and every night he wished he lived in a perfect world. One night, as he dozed, a sudden bang thundered in his ears. Once the smoke had cleared, a startled Jonny could just make out an odd-looking man sitting in the corner of his room.

'I hear you want everything to be perfect. I can make that happen, there is just one tiny price to pay, of course. You never come back to this Universe again.'

The man's voice was scratchy and irritating. Jonny was so excited he forgot about the consequences. He grabbed his bag and raced down the corridor, following the unexpected visitor.

Soon they came to a glowing square in the wall. In a breathless voice the man puffed, while pointing to the illuminated wall, 'It's just through there, where all your dreams will come true. Just remember, you only have three warnings.' And with that he shoved Jonny through the portal.

Soon Jonny found himself in a beautiful garden. It resembled his, but was flawless. He started to wander into an immaculate house. His mum (no hair out of place) ushered him to the door. But Jonny, being Jonny, had forgotten to tie his shoelace, so tumbled to the ground.

'Two warnings left,' his mum murmured; it sounded sinister.

At school Jonny got 98/100 on a mathematics test. He smiled at his friends but everybody in the room whispered ominously, 'One warning left.'

After school he played catch with his friends, but the ball hit a car. Everybody burst on to the street, chanting, 'Eliminate him!'

Jonny ran to the portal, screaming, 'They're . trying to kill me! Let me in.' The wizened man appeared, and smiling, quietly whispered, 'Perhaps you don't fit into a perfect world.'

Utopia – Daisy Stone

Jeffery is one of those boys who love their food.
Jeffery lived with his mum and dad who live in South
London and who also love their food. Jeffery doesn't
live with his parents anymore because of this:

One day I think it was last year a boy named Jeffery
set off on a school trip with all his friends to Abaton
Hill and he never came back but his friends did. Jeff
and his friends hopped on a bus from school and
spent an hour playing Top Trumps and ended off at
Millbury, by Abaton Hill, and started walking up to
the top. After ten minutes they stopped for a rest and
a snack but Jeff and his friends didn't stop, instead
they played a game of tag and ended up on the other
side of the hill, then they tried to make their way back.
The only problem was that none of them knew how
to use a compass. So on they went walking for ages
and ages until Jeff couldn't go any further because Jeff
isn't very fit so they all stopped and had an hour's rest.

Even though Jeff had friends they weren't very
good ones. After an hour they left him on the hill
alone whilst he was sleeping and carried on trying to
find their way back without him.

Meanwhile, in Jeff's head he was dreaming about a
heavenly world made out of sweets and chocolate. He
was walking down the a yellow rock road and found a
candy floss field to lay down in and think of things
that people think when they are dreaming. He
imagined that he was swimming in a pool of chocolate
surrounded by all the candy creatures bowing down to
him!

Apocalypse – Elle Binnion

It was paradise. The perfect world. Beautiful lakes and green grasses stretched as far as you could see. One day that all changed and the land was dry and bare; no life was seen for miles.

On a summer's night a girl, Jennifer, made her way down to the lake to admire a sunset that had many colours in it. She felt that something was different but thought nothing of it as everything is always perfect in the land of Utopia.

After a while she made her way back to her house and went to bed but when she woke up it was still dark. Confused, she looked at the time and it was nine o' clock. She was questioning herself when she looked outside to see all of her neighbours looking as puzzled as her. At that moment she realized that the sun was not coming up. She feared for what was to come.

Soon after she looked up to the sky and, being a clever girl, tried to figure out what was going on and then something caught her attention. The television turned on and the news was on, the headlines were 'Apocalypse Outbreak' and the news reporter was saying, 'Scientists have been expecting the end of the world but not quite as soon as this!' After the brief notice Jennifer started to panic and wondered if there was any hope. Was this really the end? Jennifer knew that she was helpless. Stuck in thought, she finally realized that this was really the end and sometimes in life things are never perfect and she never realized that her world was so perfect up until now.

Jennifer did not know what to do so she decided to just hope...she knew that there was no way she could get out of this.

The Garden Behind The Door – Freya Sinclair

Once there was a girl named Jasmine who was 10 and she was very tall for her age. She lived with her grandmother because her mum and dad were very busy people.

Her grandmother would never let her go in the garden but Jasmine didn't know why and this is where the story starts.

'Can I go out and play with my friends, Grandmother?' Jasmine asked.

'Of course you can, darling,' her Grandmother spluttered.

So off Jasmine went. But then Jasmine stopped at the door of the garden. She felt a tingle go down her spine, it felt like a mouse running across a beam. She thought to herself she just had to go into the garden to explore, so she just did that. She closed her eyes as she heard the screech of the door open and then she closed the door very quickly with a loud BANG!

She opened her big blue eyes and saw the most amazing garden in the world.

It had massive water fountains, tall monster-like trees, big colourful birds, little tweeting birds, bright green grass and beautiful flowers. Jasmine heard something, it sounded like humming so she went to investigate.

As Jasmine walked along the path to investigate the humming, she glanced across a rainbow-coloured flowerbed and saw a little bunny. 'Hello, little bunny,'

Jasmine sweetly said. But as Jasmine said that, the bunny hopped away. So Jasmine carried on walking.

As she was walking she wondered why her grandmother had kept her away from the garden, maybe because she didn't want the flowers to be trodden on, or because there is something very secret or special . in this garden.

But soon enough, as she continued on the path, Jasmine found out who was humming and she was very shocked, it was her Grandmother! She was humming a sad tune whilst standing and looking at a tomb, but who was in this old looking tomb?

Jasmine hid and looked really hard to see if there was a sign, then she looked closely at the tomb and saw a fading imprint saying *David Prichard*. That was Jasmine's grandfather's name. Jasmine gasped but then her Grandmother heard Jasmine's gasp and saw Jasmine.

'Jasmine, what are you doing here!' shouted her Grandmother.

'Um-ur,' Jasmine spluttered.

'Well just get OUT,' her grandmother exclaimed. Jasmine sprinted to the door, opened the old door and said to herself, 'I am never going in there again.'

The Apocalypse – George Hira

It was the year 2050 and a curious child named Josh was living through a horrific Apocalypse. It was caused by an evil gang of men, who wrongly thought that people with disabilities shouldn't be alive. Consequently they went round terminating all citizens who were disabled.

It was only when people realised what was happening and it was on the news they started to rebel against the idea of it. But the leader of the gang started to drug members of the public in their sleep that made them fight against the rebel and within a week a war had started.

Two weeks later and already the city of London was half blown up. One night two men snuck into Josh's room and drugged him without him knowing. When he woke up he thought that he should be fighting with the gang. So without telling his family he locked his door and crept out of the window.

When the rest of his family woke up they realised that he wasn't there because he wasn't responding when they called for him. When his dad rammed Josh's door down, he saw the open window and the empty syringe. He already knew where he was. His dad got changed and dashed over to the gang's base.

When he reached his destination, guns were firing from every angle and armed guards were surrounding the perimeter of the building. His dad scanned the building searching for an entrance but all he saw was his son, dead on the floor. His only thought was revenge.

Apocalypse – George Howard

It was pouring rain in the freezing Welsh hills. Although spring had come there was no sign of the sun. Digger's fur was soaked through and he sat on the hill shivering. All the badgers were miserable and terrified, knowing they were being targeted in the recent cull. They were trying to keep out of sight of the humans; tonight it was Digger's turn to find food.

Digger stealthily set off, running through the tunnels. He hunted for hours with nothing in sight. All the small rodents had disappeared. Why? Once or twice Digger saw a tiny mouse but that wasn't enough to feed the whole colony and anyway the mice were too fast. Then it happened, Digger poked his nose out of the tunnel and heard the piercing cry of a fellow badger. He saw two humans standing with guns in their hands laughing at the poor innocent badger they had just culled. He ran for his life. How could they be so cruel? What did the badger ever do to them? Why would they shoot the poor creature? Now that creature was lying on the ground, bloody, motionless and dead. The whole way back to his sett all Digger could think about was the badger lying dead on the ground and the humans' icy laugh made Digger's spine shiver. Something about that laugh was evil, pure evil.

Digger was exhausted and in terrible pain. When he arrived back at his sett, the whole colony had been wiped out. Bodies everywhere, no survivors. Digger was all alone and helpless. His fur, now not only soaked with water but with dripping blood. Then BANG...the lights went out.

Leaving Earth – Jacob Smith

'Please help! Help!' I cried, but they didn't listen.

Nobody listened. Sometimes I thought I was talking to myself.

So I crafted a rocket. It had to be built by the 22nd of July because I predicted 'IT' came on the 26th of July.

The rocket was 100 feet tall with a wonky yellow stripe on the side. It was called 'Leaving Earth,' and the words were etched onto the aluminium-coated wing, designed with a picture of cheetahs running up the rocket towards the curved but sharp nose.

A month later it was ready. The townsfolk thought I was out of my mind, they were so surprised that I had gone to all this effort. Even my family thought I was going mad.

On the 23rd of July the rocket blasted off. At first it sounded like thunder. Then 'woosshhh' I was surely passing the speed of sound. I was just below the clouds and the next second I was past them. The air became thin, the sky turned pitch black. I thought to myself 'this could go very wrong', but I was sure this would go right—it had to be—my life depended on it.

For the next three days I rapidly drifted a safe distance away from the Earth, then the unimaginable happened. The Sun started to expand. Mercury and Venus, the innermost planets, were devoured into the Sun's great mouth. The Sun kept getting bigger by the second, becoming brighter. The light was unbearable to look at. The star was nearly double the size that it had been originally.

Then it happened, the Sun grew until Earth was gone. Now there is no life, no people, nothing. The Apocalypse came and turned Earth into dust.

Ewe-topia – James Brewer

The day was 15th of March 2031 when the aliens' plan fell into action. They came out of their hiding places after being there for years, sneaking themselves onto the planet, making friends only to inhumanely betray them later.

All animal species and humans had been brought to a workhouse to build materials to help 'the rulers' overrun the universe and provide a military force. They were made to call them 'the rulers' as they didn't like being called aliens even though that was what they were. The rulers aimed to control everything on earth except for the clouds and what they mistook for clouds on the ground (ground clouds), sheep. This led to the sheep being the only ones not controlled and free to roam across the planet as they wished with no restrictions or orders, for them life was bliss. Fish became extinct due to no food causing them to eat each other. Insects were scarce, trees had withered and many buildings had crumbled.

Planet Two in Galaxy Nine proved a tough battle, many lives were lost including many famous people, mostly unrecognisable in their massive baggy spacesuits, faces like loons as they scattered bullets everywhere, heads covered with gigantic helmets.

The workhouse covered the whole of America, South America, Canada and parts of Greenland on to the Arctic Circle. There were four seasons, like there are today, the shortest of which was breeding, then resting where people stopped working and relaxed (this was second shortest), military season and the longest which was pure work and more work, the one that nobody liked. Military joining age was just 12.

While this carried on for many years, the work and fighting for the rulers, the sheep were having the time of their lives...so next time you're troubled, imagine you're a sheep in ewe-topia.

Apocalypse – Jessie Crabtree

I wasn't sure how long I had been knocked out. Deep, infected cuts scattered across my body. Slowly, I tried to regain my strength. Fire, destruction and death surrounded me. A huge cloud of smoke headed toward me. Quickly, finding a small brick wall on its last legs, I took shelter to stop any more dust from the toxic air getting into my lungs, and finally killing me.

The last thing I remembered was two huge hurricanes swirling above my house. I clearly recalled the walls of the next door house collapsing on my brother, for some reason I was in the garden as well. Now it seemed I was the only human to survive. My parents were away at a theatre production before disaster struck. Now there was only me left.

Once the dust cloud had cleared, I was able to haul myself up and finally get a feel for my surroundings, or lack of them. Piles of rubble lay scattered around everywhere, electric cables fizzed and smouldered and water pipes cracked. Water was soaring into the air, like a geyser.

I wondered how I would survive or keep warm. Within days I would surely to be dead or have suffered from a horrible lung disease due the acidic ash particles in my throat. I realised I had to collect the gushing water as quick as I could before the reservoir ran out.

When night came, the cold started to seep into my bones. I was starving and my stomach was rumbling more than ever. The only choice I had was to sleep on the rubble and dream of the sun rising.

On Her Own – Lucy Wadley

Loneliness is sad for a youngster especially for Sophie, a girl who doesn't enjoy life or live it to the fullest. Her mother is an alcoholic and doesn't spend much time with the poor girl. Her life is a wreck that no one cares about. All she ever dreams about is the day the perfect family will be sitting next to her.

Time went by after her dad got shot and died in the army and the only person who loved and cared about her was her dear brother. Kind and caring like a father her brother James would play and laugh with her for hours. However the day came when he joined the army and left her broken hearted with a head full of despair. Reluctant to accept the matter, Sophie would lie on the grass looking up into the night sky wondering if he would ever return.

'How could you do this to me? ' Sophie wept, gazing into her brother's eyes.

'I am fighting for what's right. I'm sorry if that affects you,' he spoke reaching for her hand.

'But I am being left with her, a woman who doesn't give a donkey's hoof about me,' she screeched, pointing her shivering finger towards her mother's beer bottle.

'I will miss you dearly but I must leave at dawn. Promise me you will try to make up with your mother and whenever you miss me look up into the stars and know I will be looking too.' James whispered reassuringly and walked off towards his bedroom.

The morning came when it was time for James to leave. Walking out onto the patio Sophie couldn't even look at her brother's waving hand. The car began moving away; tears came streaming down her face. This was the end of Sophie's world...

Utopia – Lydia Goodman

It was raining cats and dogs. Hunched against the rain, Toby Green walked hurriedly home from school. Toby was an ordinary Year 6 boy who loved to play football and hated English. Nothing exciting happened to Toby until...

The hole in the pavement suddenly appeared and Toby fell into it, whirling and twirling. Expecting to injure himself on landing, Toby was amazed to land on a thick pillow of feathers. He felt dizzy and didn't know where he was; slowly, he opened his eyes to see green all around him. He ached so much he was reluctant to move but the beautiful surroundings encouraged him to stand up and start to explore.

The beauty made Toby gasp. There were amazing diamond houses with gold-plated windows and doors. There was a school that looked outstanding with carefully decorated windows and a shiny red door. Stunning multi-coloured flowers filled the air with their gorgeous scent. Toby rubbed his eyes in disbelief as he noticed the trees were no ordinary trees, they were packed with Haribos and he reached out to fill his pockets with juicy, fruity sweets.

Suddenly, Toby heard shouting coming from behind him. It was getting closer and closer. When he turned, he saw a large figure looming over him. The figure was the most beautiful woman he had ever seen, with dazzling blue eyes, long silky blonde hair, skin as soft as a peach and ruby-red lips. However she was cross. She started to chase Toby, shouting to him that he had no right to pick the Haribo fruit from their precious trees. Toby ran and ran.

Toby sat up abruptly, dripping with sweat. What a dream...or was it, as Toby pulled from his pocket a lone Haribo sweet.

Apocalypse – Magnus McLeod

The glaring Oklahoma sun broke through the overhead canopy, scorching the already parched grass below. Hundreds of tourists flocked there weekly, searching for the picturesque forest scenes and the wildlife within.

John and Tracy, siblings, were both dressed sparsely, in T-shirt and jeans. They walked completely at ease, for their summer holiday was long and they were not restrained by chores. They were completely free to do as they pleased. The surrounding forest was awash with vibrant colours and sounds. There was an ever-present chatter and drumming of red-bellied woodpeckers and an occasional drone of hummingbirds could also be heard nearby.

They weren't far from the village they were staying in and the two relatives could still hear the bustle of activity emitted from the market. Occasional yells of prices cut through the general hubbub.

Only seconds later a terrible crash shattered the peace of the woodland. One of the tallest pines in the area splintered down its spine, throwing leaves up from the floor where it landed. An ear-splitting roar, sounding like an engine, gradually got closer to the now-terrified children.

Then several things happened simultaneously. Tracy screamed. Leaves shot in all directions, propelled by an unidentifiable force. A humanoid figure appeared in the sky directly above them. It hovered using some form of rocket attached to its metal-encased feet. A mechanical head swivelled in their direction, calculating red lights for eyes bore down on them. Freezing them in place with fear.

A booming mechanical voice echoed around the densely packed forest, scaring up the assortment of crows roosting in the treetops above.

'Surrender or be captured.'

Without so much of a glance between them, they ran. They ran, not caring where, as long as it was away from the terrifying beast laying waste to the woodland around them.

Utopia – Max Yorke Brooks

As I stepped out of my super-charged bed I felt fresh after a whole ten minutes sleep. I strutted over to the catering table, asked it for Rocky Road Clusters and they floated out of the cupboard along with the milk. I lapped all of them up greedily and asked it to clean up. A giant robot rose out of the floor with a built-in broom. While it was tidying I got a text from my friend Bob inviting me over. I got into my latest buggy, its engine was a super-charged V100, and each cylinder was three centimetres high.

One minute later, thirty miles down the road, I arrived at Bob's. He welcomed me in with a hologram of himself so I knew that he was he was in his hologram computer game. I strode in to the kit room, then, suddenly, a robot-plastered monitor's on me; pumped, I raced to find Bob. He challenged me to a game of cricket. I bowled him on twenty-five runs, his face told the whole story. A long ten minutes later we were neck and neck. He bowled the next ball then I smashed it for six runs over the boundary.

After Bob had got over his defeat, he showed me to his field where I could drive my buggy. We both zapped round his garden racecourse in negative time. It was getting dark so I thanked Bob and my buggy and I got into the Teleplonk (teleport machine). A few seconds later when I was home I asked the table for steak and chips and out came a sumptuous sizzling steak.

Apocalypse – Peter Dorrell

Utopia, meaning a perfect world. Apocalypse, meaning the end, but for some it means the exact same thing. Someone who thought that way was Fred Sinclaire. Fred had everything he could have ever dreamed of but still he wanted more. He wanted power. He was a ten-year-old boy with skinny legs and a sharp temper, yet if you ever met him you would think he was very shy. He would blush and try to hide behind his parents or whoever was with him at the time. This is the point where you realise you know this boy. You met him walking down the road on your way to work. At this point you will be wondering why this story is called Apocalypse. I'll tell you now. Fred walked along his driveway, which was probably just as big as yours, with his dog Flossy. It was then when he noticed a small orange tepee. Curious, he investigated. He slowly walked inside, cautious of its unknown contents. He suddenly heard a voice coming from the far side. 'Hello there, young one, how can I help you,' the unknown voice asked softly. For the first time since 'the incident' he stood and talked. He asked the person what they were doing on his front lawn. The unknown man ignored him and started to talk. He asked Fred what he wanted and told him that if he went away he would grant any wish. Fred told him his wish and the man handed him a sheet of paper. 'Sign here,' he said. Fred did as he said and the second he had finished he felt himself grow stronger but at the same time the world turned to rubble and there was nothing left. Fred had made the—

Utopia – Rosie Stone

Dreaming about Candy Land last night was strange but exciting. This is how it went:

'Hello, welcome to Candy Land, my name is Bobble. I'm a bubblegum bee. What's yours?' said the pink and blue striped bee, who was rather a large bee. He was the same size as my head, maybe bigger!

'Rosie,' I answered in a frightened voice because I thought he was going to sting me.

'Don't worry, I won't sting you,' said Bobble with a little giggle in his voice. 'Our type are friendly. Anyway let's get on with the tour, we don't want to be late for dinner!'

So we set off and Bobble told me everything he knew about the things we passed. There were candyfloss trees and gingerbread houses; also there was a huge chocolate lake with gingerbread families swimming in it.

After a while we came to a huge building which looked very tasty. On it in red and blue icing were the words 'MADAM CUPCAKE'S CAFE AND RESTAURANT'. I followed Bobble inside.

Behind the counter was a pretty girl with sparkly bright pink hair and she wore a dress that looked just like a cupcake.

'Hi,' said the girl cheerfully, 'my name is Daisy and I am the daughter of Madam Cupcake, what can I get for you?'

'Two smoothies and some iced buns please,' said Bobble without even asking me!

'Oh goody I love iced buns may I join you,' said Daisy excitedly. So we all sat down and ate our buns; they were delicious. Daisy wanted to join us on the tour. We left the cafe with our bellies full and carried on in the direction to Old Mother Cookie's Bakery and had dinner.

'Bang!' I'd fallen out of bed and that's how I woke up.

Apocalypse – Tamara Marsden

There was once a family of farmers who lived from
1923 to 1956 but not all of the family survived. The
family was a family of five: the farmer his wife and
their three children. They were living a wonderful war-
free life until one day came the beginning of World
War Two. The farmer and his two eldest sons were to
be sent to war. The youngest, however, was too young
to fight even though he wanted to fight beside his
father and brothers. The older brothers Ben and Ed
teased Jack (the youngest son). They said things like,
oh you'll never save your country and you'll never do
your duty for your country. Jack thought thoroughly
about what his brothers said about him and made a
plan. He wrote a letter and stuck it on the front of his
bedroom door. He packed a bag with clothes, blankets
and food and then set off before dawn.

In the morning his mother, Ruth, came to his
room to wake him up but she stopped in horror to
find a letter on his door. Ruth read it with tears in her
eyes. She told her husband Jeremy and he felt
hopeless. Two days had passed when the family
received a message the day Jeremy, Ben and Ed were
leaving. It read, Dear Mr and Mrs Thomas, I am very
sorry to say that your son Jack Thomas was lost at war
and we need three more men to take his place. He has
done very well at war and we hope to find him and
return him to you. With our deepest condolences
yours sincerely His Majesty's Government. The family
were devastated and the boys didn't go to war instead
they received a white feather.

Utopia – Tiffany Batt

It wasn't actually that long ago, in the city of Triticum Perfectionis, when an affair that would result in the biggest view change in the galaxy for over a century occurred. Triticum Perfectionis is the capital of Cinnet, one of two islands on the planet Kwezigigaba. The other island is unnamed and also slightly smaller than Cinnet. Unfortunately, this planet is not as innocent as it seems. It is a mere experiment by those humans back on Pluto. They have altered the genetics of all the inhabitants. The life of those who were living there was boring, but boredom had not been invented yet. In this world if anyone was born with a 'genetic malfunction' (which can be anything from a thought out of place) they were deported onto the other island secretly by the ruler at the time. One of the most recent cases was a child born three hours late. Thankfully, not all of the people 'deported' had a negative memory of the experience.

Chloe Wells was blind as a child and was sent away to the other island. She was seven at the time. She had silvery-blonde hair and pale blue eyes and her nose was slightly upturned. Twelve years later, when the next ship came along, she persuaded the pilot of the ship that she was dumped here by mistake. When she returned to Cinnet and moved into Triticum Perfectionis her story was written and published. In her afterword she put how life was difficult in the Other Island but all of the people stuck together like family. Despite everything it was paradise with friends.